Baby Tiger
Wants to Explore

Parent's Introduction

This book can be read with children in several different ways. You can read the book to them or, depending on their ability, they may be able to read the book to you. You can also take turns reading! Throughout the book, you will find words and phrases in big, bold text. If your child is just beginning to read, you might want to invite your child to participate in reading this text.

Your child may enjoy several readings of this story. With each reading, your child might see or focus on something new. As you read together, consider taking time to discuss the story and the information about the animals. Also, at the end of the story, we have included some fun questions to talk about together.

Baby Tiger Wants to Explore
A Photo Adventure™ Book

Concept, text and design Copyright © 2009 Leopard Learning.
Additional concepts, text and design Copyright © 2010 Treasure Bay, Inc.
Photo Adventure is a trademark of Treasure Bay, Inc. Patent No. 5,957,693.

Author	Alice Greene
Editor	Elizabeth Bennett
Publishing Director	Chester Fisher
Creative Director	Simmi Sikka
Designer	Priya Chopra
Project Manager	Shekhar Kapur
Art Editor	Maria Janet

Picture Credits
t=top b=bottom r= right l=left
Front Cover: Mistock/iStockphoto-Andre Nantel/Shutterstock
Back Cover: David A. Northcott/Corbis; Half Title: Karen Givens/iStockphoto, Aldra/iStockphoto
3 Andre Nantel/Shutterstock; 4-5 Gerard Lacz/Photolibrary; 5b Purestock/Photolibrary; 6-7 Juniors Bildarchiv/Photolibrary;
7t Chanyut Sribuarawd/iStockphoto; 8-9 Image Source/Corbis; 9t Chanyut Sribuarawd/iStockphoto;
10b Mark Schroy/iStockphoto; 10-11: D. Robert & Lorri Franz/Corbis; 12-13 David A. Northcott/Corbis; 14-15 Dlillc/Corbis;
16b Sanjeev Gupta/Shutterstock; 16-17 Mike Hill/Photographer Choice/Getty Images; 18b Dawn Nichols/iStockphoto;
18-19 Corbis/Photolibrary; 20-21 Purestock/Photolibrary; 21t: Sharon Day/Shutterstock;
22-23 Jagdeep Rajput/Photographers Direct; 24: David A. Northcott/Corbis.

Published by Treasure Bay, Inc.
P.O. Box 119, Novato, CA 94948 USA

PRINTED IN SINGAPORE

Library of Congress Catalog Card Number: 2010921694

Hardcover ISBN-10: 1-60115-287-6
Hardcover ISBN-13: 978-1-60115-287-9
Paperback ISBN-10: 1-60115-288-4
Paperback ISBN-13: 978-1-60115-288-6

Visit us online at:
www.TreasureBayBooks.com

PR 07/10

It is calm and quiet

in the **jungle.**

Suddenly, there's a rustle of leaves.

Who could it **be?**

It's a family of **tigers!**

Baby Tiger and his sister are playing with their mother.

FACT STOP

Tigers usually live in warm, thick forests. However, some tigers live in areas that are very cold and snowy.

5

FACT STOP

A baby tiger is called a *cub.*

Wait!

Baby Tiger hears something!

Is there something moving

in the **grass?**

What could it be?

7

Could it be a **bug?**

Maybe it's a mouse!

Baby Tiger hurries
off to find out.

Most tigers have orange
fur with black stripes.
Some have white fur
with black stripes.

Wait, Baby Tiger!

Your sister wants to come with **you.**

She wants to explore too!

Tiger cubs often chase each other and wrestle. This helps to make them strong.

Baby Tiger looks behind a log,
but there is nothing
there.

His sister wants to
see for herself.

12

13

Baby Tiger and his sister decide to head **back.**

Mother **Tiger** doesn't like it when they wander too far away from her.

Baby Tiger climbs up a **tree** to look for his mother. Oh, no! He can't see her! How will they know which way to **go?**

Little tiger cubs easily climb trees. Adult tigers are much heavier and prefer to stay on the ground.

Baby Tiger's sister thinks she knows the way back.

But Baby Tiger doesn't remember swimming.

FACT STOP

Most house cats don't like water, but tigers love to swim.

18

They must be **lost!**

Suddenly, the young tigers hear a roar. It's their mother! She has come looking for them, and she is **not** happy.

Tigers communicate by roaring, snarling, and moaning.

Her **cubs** should not have wandered off by themselves.

21

The sun is about to set as
Mother Tiger leads the cubs
back **home.**

The young tigers
promise to stay close
to her from now on . . .
or at least until
tomorrow!

23

Look back

through the story:

1 What is a baby tiger called?

2 Do baby tigers climb trees?

3 Do tigers like to swim?

4 Do all tigers live in forests?